This Winnie-the-Pooh
book belongs to:

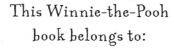

....

EGMONT

We bring stories to life

First published in Great Britain in 2012 by Egmont UK Limited
This edition published in 2016 by Egmont UK Limited
The Yellow Building, 1 Nicholas Road, London W11 4AN

Illustrated by Andrew Grey
Based on the 'Winnie-the-Pooh' works by A.A.Milne and E.H.Shepard
Illustrations © 2016 Disney Enterprises, Inc.

ISBN 978 1 4052 8191 1
51823/7
Printed in Italy

Egmont is passionate about helping to preserve the world's remaining ancient forests. We only use paper from legal and sustainable forest sources.

This book is made from paper certified by the Forest Stewardship Council® (FSC), an organisation dedicated to promoting responsible management of forest resources. For more information on the FSC, please visit www.fsc.org. To learn more about Egmont's sustainable paper policy, please visit www.egmont.co.uk/ethical.

Winnie-the-Pooh

Pooh's Christmas Adventure

EGMONT

It was a cold, snowy day in the Hundred Acre Wood. Winnie-the-Pooh watched the snowflakes fall outside his window.

"I love it when it snows," Pooh said. "But it makes me so very hungry."

Pooh decided to have his favourite snack – honey.

Wen Pooh finished eating, he looked out of the window again. Now all he could see was white. *Oh dear,* he thought. *Something is wrong with the windows.* But soon he realised he was snowed in.

"What shall I do?" he wondered.

After much thinking, Pooh had an idea.
He could use his honey-pot to dig himself out.
"All this work is making me rather hungry,"
Pooh said as he tunnelled through the snow.
"But I've run out of honey. Perhaps Piglet has some."

Pooh arrived at Piglet's house and found him snowed in, too. So Pooh used the honey-pot to dig out his friend. It took him quite a bit of time.

"Thank you," Piglet cried when Pooh finally reached Piglet's door. "You rescued me!"

"It's ... no ... bother ..." puffed Pooh, trying to catch his breath. "Do you have any honey?"

"I'm afraid not," Piglet said. "But Owl might!"

Pooh and Piglet walked to Owl's house and found that he was snowed in too.

"I suppose I'll have to dig again," Pooh sighed.

"It will be easier if we dig together," Piglet suggested.

"What a grand idea!" said Pooh.

Pooh and Piglet worked together to dig out Owl. This time, the digging went much more quickly.

"Thank you," Owl said as he opened his door. "Would you like some hot tea?"

"With honey?" Pooh asked hopefully.

After warming up inside Owl's house, the three friends went to dig out Rabbit. Things were going quite well until they heard a scratching sound.

"Whatever could that be?" Pooh asked.

"P-p-perhaps it is a Heffalump!" Piglet cried.

Suddenly Rabbit burst through the snow!
"What are you doing here?" Rabbit cried.
"We're here to dig you out," Piglet said.

"But I was coming to dig you out," Rabbit said.
"Rabbits are natural diggers, you know."

"Well, perhaps we ought to go and dig Eeyore out," Owl suggested. "With all four of us, it should take no time at all."

So Pooh, Piglet, Owl and Rabbit went to
Eeyore's house.
Everyone helped with the digging, and they
uncovered Eeyore's house in no time.
Pooh tugged on the bell rope to let Eeyore know they
were there, but it made a very peculiar sound: "Ow!"

"If I'm not mistaken," Rabbit began, "I'd say that's not a bell rope, it's Eeyore's tail!"

"I'm terribly sorry," said Pooh.

"Don't worry," Eeyore sighed. "No one bothers about me anyway."

"But, Eeyore," Piglet explained, "we've just rescued you!"

"And now that you've been rescued, let's see if Christopher Robin needs our help," Owl said.

Pooh, Piglet, Owl, Rabbit and Eeyore came upon Christopher Robin in the forest.

"Are you stuck? Shall we help dig you out?" asked Pooh. "We're really quite good at it."

"I'm not stuck, you silly old Bear!" laughed Christopher Robin. "I'm making a snowman!"

"A snowman?" Pooh asked curiously. "How do you make one of those?"

"I'll show you," Christopher Robin said. "If we all work together, it'll be an even better one!"

So Christopher Robin, Pooh and Rabbit helped to roll a giant snowball for the snowman's body. Eeyore found stones to use for the snowman's face. Piglet searched for twigs to use as arms, and Owl flew them into place.

"This is the grandest snowman I've ever seen!" Christopher Robin said. "And I couldn't have done it without all of you!"

The End.

Enjoy the classic tales about
Winnie-the-Pooh and friends!

ISBN 978 1 4052 7938 3

ISBN 978 1 4052 7940 6